TRICK OR TREAT
FROM THE
BLACK LAGOON®

Get more monster-sized laughs from

The Black Lagoon®

TRICK OR TREAT
FROM THE
BLACK LAGOON®

by Mike Thaler
Illustrated by Jared Lee

SCHOLASTIC INC.

For Tom, Jewel, Han & Sam
—M.T.

To Gary Quint
—J.L.

Text Copyright © 2015 by Mike Thaler
Illustrations Copyright © 2015 by Jared Lee

ISBN 978-0-545-85072-8

10 9 8 7 6 5 4   15 16 17 18 19 20/0

Printed in the U.S.A.   40
First printing 2015

GAWKY
GNATS
↓

FRISKY
FLEAS
↓

CONTENTS

TERRIFIED
COOTIES

CHAPTER 1
TAKING A FALL

It's fall again. I think they call it fall because everything falls. Leaves fall, rain or snow fall, and the thermometer falls. But the scariest part of fall is Halloween.

And the scariest part of Halloween is trick-or-treating.

Going out on that night, you might bump into Frankenstein's monster, Count Dracula, or even Godzilla. And if you survive, you wind up with a stomachache and some new cavities.

CHAPTER 2
UP IN DISGUISE

Halloween is three days away. At school, all of my friends are pretty excited about it. Eric is going as the Wolfman. He says he wants to trim his dog and stick all the hair on his face with Scotch tape. I hope he doesn't get fleas.

FLEAS→

Derek is going as Count Dracula. He has plastic fangs and a black tablecloth for a cape. Freddy is going as a giant lamb chop. Doris is going as a ballet dancer. It's tutu bad. Girls have no sympathy for monsters. Penny is going as a lawyer. Actually, they're pretty scary.

I have no idea what my costume will be. I know I don't want to be a monster. There are enough scary things in the world already.

CHAPTER 3

A PEEP INTO THE PAST

When I get home, I ask Mom if she has any ideas.

"One year, when I was a little girl, I wore a Bo Peep costume," she says.

MOM, CAN WE TALK?

"Did you lose all your sheep?" I ask.

"Yes, but I found a lot of candy instead."

13

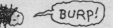

Mom even has an old photo that Grandma had taken of her. It's hard to imagine Mom trick-or-treating. She says she loved candy when she was little. I still wish she did when we're at the supermarket.

PARTY STORE

WIGS · COSTUMES.
FUNNY SHOES.
GAMES AND MUCH
MORE

AWESOME!

She suggests we go to a party store because they have every costume you could ever imagine.

Mom's right. The costume store has it all. You can be any superhero or any villain. You can be Luke Skywalker or Darth Vader. Why would anyone want to be Darth Vader? He was a bad dude. Bad dudes seem to be popular these days. The badder the better . . . I don't get it. How are we going to make a better world if it's full of bad dudes?

I LIKE THIS ONE.

COOL.

Each costume costs a lot. It would take my whole allowance to be a mummy. I won't get wrapped up in that. Maybe I'll just get a red ball nose for seventy-five cents and be a clown. All the world loves a clown.

CHAPTER 5
BRING ON THE CLOWNS

Well, I have half my costume. Now I need the rest. I could put on Mom's tennis shoes. She's got pretty big feet. If I put a pillow on my stomach, and one in the back of my pants, I might get a laugh. I look like Mrs. Beamster!

MRS. BEAMSTER, THE LIBRARIAN

Mom found red suspenders at a garage sale. I'm glad she didn't buy the whole garage. With my red nose, I think I'm about ready to rock.

21

CHAPTER 6
CLOWNING AROUND

THE BULLY →

GRRRR...

The big night is tomorrow. Everyone on the bus home from school is excited. The class bully is looking forward to playing tricks on everyone: turning over garbage cans, spraying shaving cream in mailboxes, and putting toilet paper on porches. I hope someone does it to his house, so he sees how it feels.

YOU'RE IN THE WRONG BOOK.

As for me, I'm looking forward to being funny. I have memorized a bunch of monster jokes to ask folks.

HUBIE'S MONSTER JOKES

Why are cemeteries so crowded?
Because everyone's dying to get in.

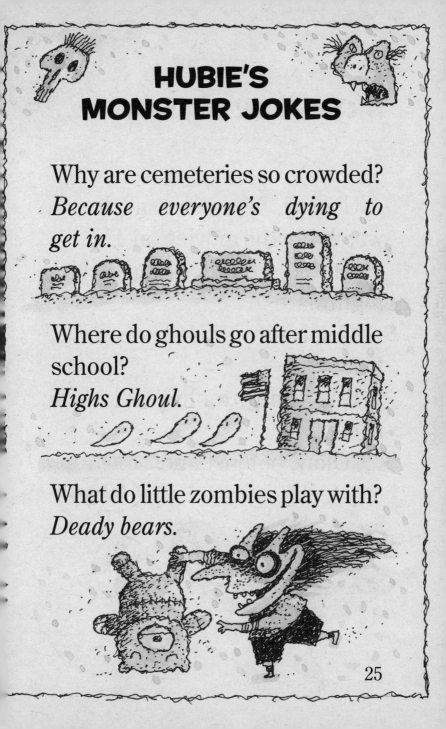

Where do ghouls go after middle school?
Highs Ghoul.

What do little zombies play with?
Deady bears.

CHAPTER 7
MONSTER MANIA

Usually, Mom doesn't let me watch horror movies on TV.

"Hubie, you're going to have nightmares."

"Aw, Mom, it's Halloween eve," I say.

But tonight she makes an exception.

"Okay, but just one."

"Deal."

HEY!

I have my pick from a whole bunch of monsters. There is *Frankenstein, Frankenstein Returns, Frankenstein in Love, Frankenstein at the Beach*, and *Frankenstein Plays Pro Football*.

There are also vampires, ghosts, wolfmen, and more monsters. I pick *The Mummy Returns*. I thought it might be about a dead pharaoh returning overdue books to the library.

I cover my eyes, but peek out a little. The mummy has no nose. I wonder if he still catches colds. And it is very clear that the mummy hasn't brushed his teeth in 2,000 years.

30

COULD YOU CALL ME A TAXI?

YOU'RE A TAXI.

In the movie, the archaeologist searching for the mummy is brushing his teeth before going to bed. When he looks in the mirror, he sees the mummy behind him getting closer, and closer, and closer . . . and that's when I decide to turn off the television, brush my teeth, and go to bed. I check twice in the mirror for mummies but all I see is a mommy checking on me.

CHAPTER 9
INSTANT REPLAY

That night, guess what? I have . . . a nightmare. Why are moms always right?

In my dream I'm out trick-or-treating with Eric. We come to an old house.

"Let's go," I say, turning around.

"Let's go in," says Eric.

"That's what I meant," I say.

I'M SCARED OF EVERYTHING.

"You   chicken?"   asks   Eric,
slowly stepping in.

"Not   me,"   I   say,   following
slowly.

We continue down the hall.

"I hope they don't give us apples," says Eric.

"Or Brussels sprouts," I add.

At the end of the hall we come to a door. There's a scary sign on it.

"Let's go," I whisper.

"Cluck, cluck," says Eric.

The door slowly opens and out steps a . . .

Luckily, I wake up before I see the monster and vow never to watch another horror movie.

RUBBER ← COTTON

CHAPTER 10
A COOL SCHOOL GHOUL

COSTUME

SNACK

The next day, Mrs. Green's classroom is decorated with rubber spiders and cotton spiderwebs. Mrs. Green has on a *Creature from the Black Lagoon* costume. At least I think it's a costume. Well, anyway, that day there's not much work . . . but lots of fun.

IN REVERSE

PAPER EAR

PAPER CLOWN CAP

PAPER EAR

APPLE

COOKIE

We bob for apples, eat chocolate chip witch cookies, do puzzles, make masks in art class, and I make a paper clown's cap and big paper ears. When we visit the library, Mrs. Beamster has out all the Halloween books. Then she reads to us the history of Halloween.

40

MRS. BEAMSTER →

CHAPTER 11
THE HISTORY OF HALLOWEEN

We learn that the holiday of Halloween has been celebrated since ancient times. It started out as a festival celebrating the end of the summer harvest and the beginning of the winter season.

THE FIELDS ARE HARVESTED.

LET'S PARTY.

This festival was first known as Samhaim (pronounced Sah-win), then later as All Hallows' Eve, which evolved into Hallowe'en, and eventually Halloween.

The traditional activities—trick-or-treating, costume parties, visiting haunted houses, and carving jack-o'-lanterns—are now celebrated every October 31, by children all over the world.

It is still a harvest festival, I think. A harvest of candy!

43

CHAPTER 12
A HAIRY ENCOUNTER

Halloween eve is finally here! My mom is full of advice.

"Don't take unwrapped candy. Don't go in a house if you don't know the people. And never talk to strangers."

OK, MOM.

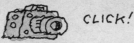
CLICK!

I listen carefully. Moms are always right. Then she takes a picture of me that I can show to my kid one day. I'm scared and excited as I head down the block.

The first monster I meet is the Wolfman. He definitely needs a shave. I pretend to be scared.

"It's only me," smiles Eric.

"Boy, you had me fooled," I say. "Your costume's a howl. How's your dog?"

"Bald," says Eric.

45

"Knock, knock," I say.

"Who's there?" asks Eric.

"Howl."

"Howl who?" asks Eric.

"Howl I get in, if you don't open the door." I laugh and we continue down the street.

TASTY TREAT

CHAPTER 13
YOU CAN COUNT ON ME

The next monster we meet is Dracula.

"I vant to suck your blood," says the count.

47

"Derek, don't be a pain in the neck."

"But I like your type."

"I'm type O positive," I say.

"Oh, maybe I'll try the folks' necks door."

HAPPY SKULL

The folks next door are the Joneses. Their house is the most decorated on the block. They have skeletons with blinking red eyes, laughing witches on broomsticks, and a lawn full of tombstones. Nobody ever keeps up with the Joneses.

Derek rings the doorbell. Mrs. Jones comes to the door dressed like the Bride of Frankenstein. "Trick or treat!" we shout.

"How cute you all look," she says. "What are you supposed to be?" she smiles, turning to Derek.

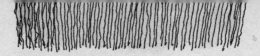

"I'm Count Dracula, a vampire, and I vant to suck your blood."

"Ohh, I'm scared," smiles Mrs. Jones. "Would you settle for an all-day sucker?"

"What flavor?" asks Derek.

"Tonight we have strawberry, lemon, and blueberry lollipops."

"I'll take the strawberry," says the count.

"Lemon," says Eric.

"Blueberry and thank you," I say.

COME CLOSER, CHILDREN.

53

"Thank you," says Eric.

"Thenk yuuu," lisps the count.

We walk down the street licking our all-day suckers.

"I vonder if these are all-night suckers, too?" asks the count.

54

CHAPTER 14

WITCH SWITCH

HI, GUYS.

WHERE DID YOU GET THOSE SUCKERS?

A little farther down the block we meet the girls. Doris is in a pink tutu and Penny is dressed like a witch.

← KAT

↑ SPELLED WRONG

55

"I thought you were going to be a lawyer?" I say.

"All the lawyer costumes were sold out," she answers.

"Oh, too bad," I say.

"Not so bad," says Penny. "This is a close second."

We all trick-or-treat together and in an hour each of us has a large assortment of candy, gum, fruit, popcorn, lollipops, and quarters. Mine is all stuck together in a giant ball.

"It looks like a planet of cavities," says Penny. "I kept all mine separate."

"It all goes together in your stomach," says Eric.

"Gross," say the girls, and they walk away.

We eat our entire candy haul. In an hour it is all gone except for the quarters. The three of us are very green.

"I don't feel so good," says Dracula.

"I really don't, either," says the Wolfman.

"I wanna go home," I say, holding my pillow.

"There's still two more blocks in the neighborhood," says Dracula.

OOOHHH....

I FEEL TERRIBLE.

MY STOMACH IS TURNING.

Just then Freddy comes up. He is a giant lamb chop.

"Hey, guys, let's go to my house. My mom has cake and ice cream waiting for us."

I'M HAVING A BALL! HOW ABOUT YOU GUYS?

TREATS

I'M DIZZY.

The three of us make a sound that is a cross between a gag, a groan, and a grunt! We turn three shades greener.

GREEN

GREENER

"And Mom will love your costumes. Those are the best Hulk outfits I've ever seen," smiles Freddy.

And indeed they were.

COOL.

GREENEST

PS: I guess when mummies eat too much candy, they get tomb-y aches.